The Great Escape

W9-CGV-257

SUSAN AKASS

ILLUSTRATED BY LOMA TILDERS

Rigby

Contents

CHAPTER ONE

Magic

Catherine Young wanted a hamster. She wasn't quite sure why she wanted one so badly. Partly it was because her cousin Mikey had one. Partly it was because she was a bit like a hamster herself, or so Mikey said. She was small and quick, with bright eyes. And partly it was because she had no brothers or sisters. A hamster would be someone to talk to.

She asked her dad. "Please, Dad, can I have a hamster?"

Dad replied, "I don't think it would be very wise, do you, Catherine?"

And Catherine sadly agreed that it wouldn't be very wise at all.

The problem was Tiger, their cat. Tiger was a long, lean tabby cat who was as fearsome as his name. He was a deadly hunter. Catherine knew that no hamster would be safe with Tiger in the house.

But still she wanted a hamster, and she couldn't stop talking about it.

On Catherine's eighth birthday, she ran downstairs to find a large cardboard box on the kitchen table. She couldn't imagine what was in it. She picked it up. It was lighter than she had expected. She was about to shake it when Mom said, "Don't do that! It's fragile!"

Puzzled, Catherine peeled back the sticky tape and looked inside. There she saw a round, plastic tank and a maze of curved red and yellow tubes.

Catherine knew exactly what it was—a hamster cage. The tubes fit together to make tunnels and runs. There was a wheel for the hamster to exercise in.

Catherine lifted the cage out of the box. At the bottom, in the soft, yellow bedding, Catherine could just make out a tiny ball of golden brown fur. She couldn't believe her eyes. She turned to her parents, "What about Tiger?" she asked.

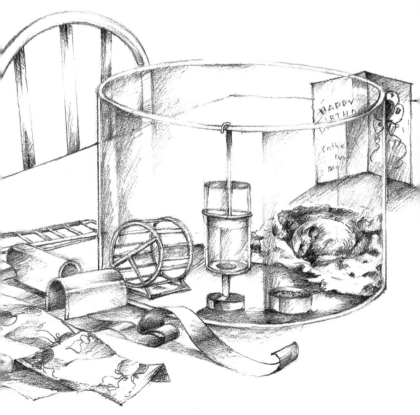

"You wanted a hamster so much, we decided to risk it," replied Dad. "But you'll have to keep him in your room and always remember to shut the door."

"I will," said Catherine, nodding her head confidently.

Very quietly, Catherine began to talk to the hamster.

"You're magic," she whispered, "and that's going to be your name. Magic!" Carefully, she opened the cage and slipped her hand inside. Gently, she cupped it around the tiny creature and lifted him out of the cage.

The hamster uncurled in Catherine's hand, and stood staring at her with bright black eyes. His nose and

whiskers twitched. His tiny feet tickled
her hand. Catherine held out her
other hand and Magic began to run
from one to the other. Catherine was
entranced.

"He's perfect!" she exclaimed. "Thanks a million!"

"Don't handle him too much today," said Mom. "He's only a baby, and he needs to get used to you."

Hamsters sleep during the day, so when Catherine went to bed that night, Magic was just waking up.

Catherine lay in bed watching Magic scampering through the tunnels and running on the wheel. She watched him filling his cheeks with food until they looked as if they would burst. The wheel squeaked, his footsteps pattered, his teeth gnawed. Catherine wondered if all the noise would keep her awake. It didn't.

CHAPTER TWO

Tiger Waits

Catherine's love for Magic didn't wear off. She never forgot to feed him, or change the water in his bottle, or clean out his cage. She played with him each day after school, and she always remembered to close her bedroom door.

But Tiger knew that there was something going on in Catherine's room. He could smell the hamster.

10

He lurked outside and waited for his chance.

It came one terrible Saturday. Dad was out shopping. Mom was downstairs baking a cake. Catherine was upstairs playing with Magic. Suddenly, there was a loud crash and a scream from Mom. Catherine quickly put Magic back into the cage and ran downstairs.

Mom was sitting on the floor holding her ankle. She had been standing on a rickety old chair, reaching for the raisins when the chair had collapsed. There was flour and sugar everywhere, and Mom's ankle was already swelling.

"If you lean on me, can you hop to the couch?" asked Catherine.

"I think so," Mom gasped, and taking Catherine's hand, she pulled herself up. They made it to the couch.

"I'll get an ice pack," Catherine said, and she ran back to the kitchen.

As she walked in, she saw footprints in the flour ... cat's footprints. Dark in the whiteness of the flour, then white on the wooden floor, they led out of the kitchen and across the hall toward the stairs.

"No!" cried Catherine. She sprinted for her bedroom, but it was too late. The door was open, the hamster cage was in pieces on the floor, and there was no sign of Magic. Desperately, Catherine searched the room—under the bed, under the dresser, in her toy box.

At that moment, Dad came home. "I'm back!" he called cheerfully.

Brushing her tears away, Catherine went back into action. She hadn't even gotten the ice pack yet. Now she and Dad would have to take Mom to the hospital for an X-ray. There wasn't time to think about Magic.

Catherine kept her sadness tight inside her the whole time that they were at the hospital getting Mom's broken ankle put in a cast. She kept it under control when they arrived home. Then Dad asked her to feed Tiger, and the tears wouldn't stop.

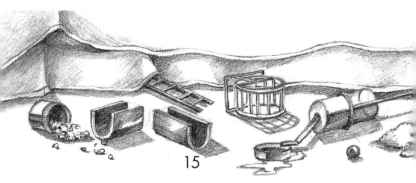

Dad was mystified. "What's the matter, Catherine?" he asked as she sobbed and sobbed. At last, Catherine gasped it out.

"M-m-magic," she sobbed. "Tiger got Magic. I ran downstairs when Mom fell, and I didn't close the door!"

"Oh, Catherine!" cried Mom. "Are you sure that Tiger caught him?"

Catherine nodded. "He knocked Magic's cage over. Magic wouldn't have had a chance."

"No," agreed Mom sadly. "He was only a baby. He wouldn't have had a chance." Mom thought for a few moments, and then asked, "Would it help if I promised to buy you another hamster?"

Catherine shook her head. "It wouldn't be the same," she sobbed.

CHAPTER THREE

With Magic Gone

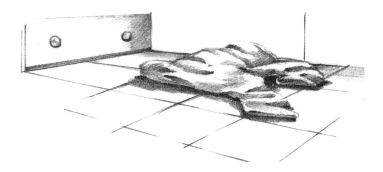

All the next morning, Catherine hung around the yard, kicking a soccer ball and trying not to think of Magic. Then it began to rain, and feeling cold and miserable, she went back inside. One of her old sweaters was lying on the floor in the corner of the kitchen. Catherine pulled it on and went to see how Mom was.

As she walked into the living room, Mom exclaimed, "Catherine! What have you done to that sweater?"

Catherine looked down. There were three big holes on one side of it.

"I don't know. It was fine last time I wore it."

"You must have caught it on something," suggested Mom. Catherine couldn't remember catching it on anything, but she shrugged and agreed.

Catherine sat down and began to read a book. Mom was bored and restless.

"Get me the newspaper, please, Catherine," she asked. Catherine brought in the newspaper from the kitchen.

Her mother unfolded it and exclaimed, "How strange! There are holes in this, too!"

Catherine looked up. Her mother was looking at her through a hole in the middle of the paper. She laughed, but thought no more of it.

Just then her dad called.

"Catherine, come and peel some potatoes for lunch."

"Coming!"

Catherine wasn't much good at peeling potatoes, but she knew she had to help. She took out some large potatoes from the vegetable rack.

"Strange," she thought, as she started on the first one. "There are holes in this, too." As she looked more closely, she thought, "Those look like tooth marks! I wonder ..." but she hardly dared to let herself think about it anymore.

Instead, she dropped the peeler. She knelt down to pick it up, and gazed around the kitchen floor. There was a narrow gap under the cabinets. Was it big enough? Catherine thought so.

"Dad," she said, in a small, hopeful voice. "Something has been nibbling things in this kitchen. Something nibbled my sweater, something nibbled the paper, and something nibbled this potato. Do you think it was Magic?"

Dad looked down at the potato.

Then gently he said, "I don't see how it could be Magic, Catherine. How could he ever have gotten away from a hunter like Tiger? And how could he have gotten down from your room without Tiger spotting him? No, it's probably just a wild mouse. Tiger will catch it tonight."

Silently, Catherine went back to peeling potatoes, but she wasn't convinced.

"It could be Magic," she thought, "and if it is, I've got to find him before Tiger does."

CHAPTER FOUR

Watching in the Night

Catherine knew that if Magic was alive, he wouldn't come out in the daytime. He would be curled up somewhere in a nest made of yarn and newspaper. But he'd be looking for food as soon as it got dark.

Catherine began to think. Tiger always went out at night, but he could get back in through his cat flap. If she locked the cat flap so he couldn't get in, Magic would be safe. Then later, when Mom and Dad were asleep, she would come down and search for Magic. First she would have to shut the cat flap without Dad noticing.

That evening, just before bedtime, Catherine went to get a glass of milk from the kitchen. Dad was watching TV and didn't suspect anything. Quietly, Catherine closed the catch on the cat flap. Then she ran upstairs to go to bed.

"I won't go to sleep," she said to herself as she lay down. "I'll stay awake and save Magic."

In the middle of the night, Catherine woke up suddenly. She was angry at herself for falling asleep, but it didn't matter—she was awake now.

She picked up a flashlight and tip-toed down to the kitchen. She shined it around in the dark. Immediately, Catherine saw what had woken her up. The metal vegetable rack had been knocked over. It was lying on the floor surrounded by potatoes, carrots, and onions.

She swung the flashlight around. It lit up two green, glowing eyes. Tiger! He must have knocked over the vegetable rack. How had he gotten in again? Dad must have opened the cat flap.

As Catherine watched, Tiger heard a sound. He tensed, a hunter ready to spring.

"No!" shouted Catherine and tackled him just as he pounced. Tiger hissed and scratched and yowled, but Catherine didn't care. She clutched him tightly around his middle and shoved him through the cat flap, out into the night. Then once again, she closed the catch.

Outside the door, Tiger yowled angrily. Catherine ignored him. She was searching under the cabinets with her flashlight—searching for a pair of beady, black eyes and a small, golden body. She saw nothing.

She found the box of hamster food and poured a little of it near the place where Tiger had pounced. Then she took a couple of grapes from the fruit bowl. They were Magic's favorite food. She held on to them and sat back to watch and wait.

The minutes passed slowly. Tiger gave up yowling. Upstairs, her parents were still asleep.

Catherine's eyes began to close. She jerked them open again and again. The last time, she slept a little longer. As she woke, she heard a tiny sound— a nibbling sound. She opened her eyes, and there, a few inches from her feet, was Magic. He was sitting up, daintily nibbling on a piece of corn.

At first, Catherine didn't move a muscle. She just began to talk in the low, gentle voice she always used with Magic.

"Come here, Magic. Good boy, Magic."

Magic was used to her and wasn't afraid. Catherine held the grapes and inched her open hand toward Magic. Then she held it still.

Magic stopped nibbling and sniffed the air. His nose and whiskers twitched, and his head turned as he tried to locate the delicious smell. Then in an instant, Catherine felt the prickle of Magic's tiny feet on her palm. Catherine let him take a grape, and then she closed her fingers firmly around Magic's warm, soft body.

Catherine didn't tell her parents until the next morning. They were still in bed, half asleep, when she ran in to tell them of Magic's magical escape.

"And I hope we never get robbed," she added, when they had all hugged each other with excitement. "Because if robbers got in, you two would never hear them in a million years!"

That day, Dad bought a huge plastic fish tank. He drilled a couple of holes in the bottom and screwed it to the top of Catherine's table. It was large enough for Magic's cage to fit inside, and Catherine could still watch Magic through its transparent sides. There was no way that Tiger could ever knock THAT off. There would never again be a great escape!